Edward
the
African Grey Bush
Elephant

Pauline Westgate

AuthorHouse™ UK
1663 Liberty Drive
Bloomington, IN 47403 USA
www.authorhouse.co.uk
UK TFN: 0800 0148641 (Toll Free inside the UK)
UK Local: 02036 956322 (+44 20 3695 6322 from outside the UK)

This book is printed on acid-free paper.

ISBN: 978-1-6655-8502-6 (sc)
ISBN: 978-1-6655-8501-9 (e)

Print information available on the last page.

Published by AuthorHouse 01/30/2021

authorHOUSE®

Edward

the
African Grey Bush
Elephant

Once there was a shy grey bush elephant who lived in Africa amongst the tall trees and bushes in which he kept himself hidden, all that you could ever see was the tip of his trunk and one eye.

Edward became shy when he lost his troop and he was young and wasn't sure which way he should go to find them, so he thought it would be better to stay where he was, and hope that the troop or his mother would come back for him.

As time went on and days passed Edward the shy grey elephant began to wonder how he would be able to cope on his own, this made him very tired and worried. As he was thinking to himself he fell fast asleep.

The shy grey elephant began to dream for his family, in the dream he was trying to look for them, a little tear began to fall from Edward's eye, as he dreamt of his mother and his troop.

Then suddenly Edward felt the ground vibrating, and something could be heard. Was it a stampede or was it thunder the shy grey elephant wondered what it was, then Edward the elephant didn't know what this terrible noise was, he started to shake and he used his ears to cover his eyes, he was so frightened.

He moved one of his ears back to peep out to see if there was anything happening or was it a dream.

But no it was a rumble of the feet of his troop, oh how wonderful that his troop, his family and his mother came back for him, when Edward the shy grey elephant realised this, he blow down his trunk and made the loudest squeakiest noise that anyone had ever heard from a baby elephant before.

His mother then returned his squeaky noise with a huge trumpet sound. His mother rushed over to him and made a fuss, the shy grey elephant rubbed up against his mother and his mother rubbed her trunk up and down his body they were so excited to see each other and the troop began to make a fuss of the shy grey elephant. And his mother told Edward he was to never leave her side again.

Now Edward was back with his mother and his troop he was very happy, he brushed away the tear and begun to have fun with the troop he thought he had lost, he followed close to his mother and the rest of the troop, they took him to a watering hole where the shy grey elephant drank the water and wallowed in the wet mud, the shy grey elephant was having a lovely time.

Then the matriarch of the troop let out the largest loudest noise to tell the troop they were off and to make sure everyone follows, the matriarch lead the troop and each elephant followed in turn holding onto the tail in front of them, Edward's mother made sure her baby was with her.

Edward slowly grew and lost his shyness and got bigger and taller. The grey elephant with big long tusks stayed with the troop until he became a father himself.

When Edwards baby elephant was born he was so proud, and once Edward's baby was big enough, he told her the story of how he had got lost and how lonely he felt until they found him, so again Edward said how important it is to stay close to her parents and the troop.

Printed in the United States
By Bookmasters